RE

One Back

13-12-17

worcestershire
countycouncil
Libraries & Learning

FOR DAVID GILL AND ALL AT THE
SOUTH LAKES WILD ANIMAL PARK
WHO WORK SO HARD TO SAVE
TIGERS FROM EXTINCTION – JB & SV

STRIPES PUBLISHING
An imprint of Magi Publications
1 The Coda Centre, 189 Munster Road,
London SW6 6AW

A paperback original
First published in Great Britain in 2009

Text copyright © Jan Burchett and Sara Vogler, 2009
Illustrations copyright © Diane Le Feyer of Cartoon Saloon, 2009
Cover illustration copyright © Andrew Hutchinson, 2009

ISBN: 978-1-84715-052-3

A CIP catalogue record for this book is available
from the British Library.

Printed and bound in Germany.

10 9 8 7 6 5 4 3 2 1

CHAPTER ONE

"That's got to be the weirdest present I've ever had!" said Ben.

A shiny glass eyeball was glaring at him from its brown envelope.

"The weirdest present *we've* ever had. It's my birthday too," his twin sister Zoe reminded him. "Who's it from?"

"Dunno," said Ben. He shook the eyeball out of the envelope. It was the size of a small marble, yellow flecked with a black dot.

Zoe took the envelope and pulled out a piece of paper with a printed message.

"Happy Eleventh Birthday, Zoe and Ben," she read. "But it's not signed."

"This is one of your jokes, isn't it?" Ben grinned, waving the marble in her face.

His sister shook her head, flicking her brown hair out of her eyes. "I don't know anything about it."

"Yeah, right!"

"No honest!" insisted Zoe. "I've never seen it before."

"Perhaps Mum and Dad sent it," said Ben.

"We've had their presents already," said Zoe. She studied the envelope more closely. "Anyway, it's not a Mexican stamp."

Ben and Zoe's parents were vets who travelled the world working with endangered animals. A month ago they'd been posted to Mexico on a project to protect the critically endangered Chiapan Climbing Rat. Ben and Zoe had always gone with them in the past. But in

September they would be starting secondary school so their parents had decided they had to stay in England. Mum and Dad kept them up to date with regular phone calls, but it wasn't the same as being there. Gran had come to look after them while their parents were away, and at this moment she was clattering about in the kitchen, icing a birthday cake.

Ben held up the eyeball. "Maybe it's a clue to something," he said. "Like in those treasure hunts Mum and Dad used to do for us."

"It's not much of a clue though," said Zoe, frowning. "What do we do next?"

"Maybe the sender has left a message on our website," said Ben. "That's how most people get in touch with us." He pocketed the glass eyeball, went to the computer and logged in. A picture of a gorilla filled the screen, with the words "animals in danger" arched over its head. The deep cry of a silverback male echoed round the room.

During their travels with their parents Ben and Zoe regularly posted updates of their projects on their website. And they also used it to keep in touch with the people they'd met all over the world.

"There's loads of new posts," said Ben. He scrolled down.

"There's one from the Elephant Sanctuary in Kenya," said Zoe. "Open it up. Awwww, Zahara had a bull calf this morning!"

A photo of a tiny baby elephant with huge ears and a tufty topknot flashed up on the screen.

"Cute," gushed Zoe. "And he shares our birthday."

Ben rolled his eyes and quickly scrolled down the list. He was just as keen to protect animals as his sister, but sometimes she hit the jackpot on the Gooey Scale.

"There's one from Brian and his orang-utans."

"I don't recognize the one below it," said Zoe. "It says The Island."

Ben clicked on it. "You'll have got the eye by now," he read slowly. "Time to give it back to its rightful owner. Then the adventure can begin."

"Adventure?" said Zoe. "What adventure?"

Ben pulled the eyeball out of his pocket. "Better do as we're told. But who's lost a glass eye?"

"Looks like a cat's," said Zoe thoughtfully. "But there's no one-eyed cat round here!"

"It's not a cat's eye," Ben said. "They don't have round pupils, more of a slit." Suddenly he jumped to his feet and made for the door. "I've got it! Come on!"

Zoe caught up with him by the bookshelf in the hall. He was wobbling on a chair, reaching for the very top. He pulled down an ugly china tiger, which Gran had brought with her when she came to stay. She'd insisted on it being displayed in spite of protests from the rest of the family.

The tiger was battered and chipped and had one yellow glass eye. The other was missing, leaving only an empty socket.

Ben and Zoe looked at each other.

"So did Gran set the puzzle?" said Ben.

"Put it in and we'll find out," urged Zoe.

Ben took the eyeball and pressed it into the socket. It fitted perfectly.

There was a click and a whir and the
three-dimensional image of a man appeared
in the air. "A hologram!" exclaimed Zoe.

"Greetings, Godchildren," said the image, with a jovial smile. "Of course, if you're not Ben and Zoe Woodward this message isn't for you."

"It's Uncle Stephen!" gasped Ben. "But he disappeared four years ago!"

Their godfather, Dr Stephen Fisher, a world-renowned animal specialist, had vanished at around the time of their seventh birthday and hadn't been heard of since. Ben and Zoe hadn't seen him often, but they'd always looked forward to his visits. And, of course, they'd never missed a single one of his TV appearances. They'd loved their godfather and his crazy ways. He would make up clever games that always had them thinking hard and howling with laughter at the same time.

"As you know, I disappeared some time ago," said the flickering image. "This is my hologram. That doesn't mean I'm dead, far from it. I went undercover so I could concentrate on my great plan to save endangered animals."

The image stepped right up to them.

"I'm going to tell you a secret." He looked around as if to make sure no one was listening. Ben and Zoe found themselves doing the same. "Four years ago, I set up an organization called Wild – which must remain completely confidential!"

"Why's he telling us about it then?" hissed Ben.

"I expect you're wondering why I'm telling you about it," Uncle Stephen went on brightly. "I've kept an eye on your movements and I'm very impressed with your work with endangered animals. You both have valuable skills and knowledge and I want you to join me at Wild. Can't tell you where it is, of course, but your contact will be in touch. See you soon!"

The image flickered. Then it appeared again. "Erm … if you're not Ben and Zoe Woodward, then obviously your contact won't be in touch," it said apologetically and vanished.

"Wow!" gasped Ben. "A secret organization – and Uncle Stephen wants us to join. We'd better get packed."

"Hang on," said Zoe. "You're always rushing into things. We don't know where we're going yet, or who our contact is."

"Children!" Gran was yelling from the kitchen. "Cake's ready."

"We'll talk later," said Ben. "I'm not missing Gran's chocolate cake for anything!"

They raced down the hall to the kitchen. Gran stood beaming at them, holding out a chocolate cake with eleven candles. She winked at them.

"Just got time for this before your Wild adventure."

CHAPTER TWO

Ben and Zoe rattled along in the back of Gran's little car.

"I can't get my head round this, Gran," said Ben. "You were in on our godfather's secret all along."

"As soon as Stephen contacted me I knew you two would be perfect to join Wild." Gran smiled.

"And you won't tell us any more."

"Certainly not!" declared Gran. "That's up to him."

She suddenly swung the car off the road

and started to drive across a field! Zoe
looked at Ben. "Has Gran lost her marbles?"
she whispered. The car was lurching wildly
over the furrowed ground.

"Nearly there," called their grandmother
over her shoulder.

Now the children could see a helicopter
in the field ahead. A young woman jumped
out. She was wearing jeans and a thick
jacket and her blonde hair was tied in a
rough ponytail.

"That's Erika," said Gran. "She'll be
taking you from here." She bumped the car
to a halt. "Have fun and be safe," she said,
blowing them a quick kiss as they got
out. "And don't worry about your
mum and dad. I'll deal with
them. See you soon."
She hurtled off
across the
field.

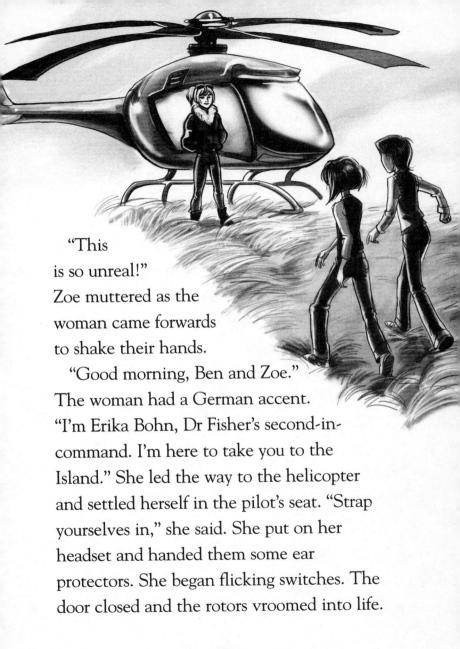

"This
is so unreal!"
Zoe muttered as the
woman came forwards
to shake their hands.

"Good morning, Ben and Zoe."
The woman had a German accent.
"I'm Erika Bohn, Dr Fisher's second-in-command. I'm here to take you to the
Island." She led the way to the helicopter
and settled herself in the pilot's seat. "Strap
yourselves in," she said. She put on her
headset and handed them some ear
protectors. She began flicking switches. The
door closed and the rotors vroomed into life.

"Where are we going?" asked Ben, shouting above the noise.

"Any questions will have to wait for Dr Fisher," Erika told them as they flew north over fields and towns. "He's bursting to tell you all about it himself and would never forgive me if I let anything slip."

Zoe sniffed the air. "What's that smell? Is everything all right with the helicopter?"

Erika chuckled. "I forgot to warn you. We use alternative energy sources at Wild. This helicopter is fuelled by chicken manure."

"You mean *poo?*" said Ben.

"Yes," said Erika. "It's environmentally friendly. And free – there's plenty on the Island. But it does take a while to get used to the smell."

Now they'd left the land behind and were flying over choppy waves.

"Landing in thirty seconds," Erika announced.

"Where?" whispered Zoe.

"Look, there's a little island ahead," Ben told her, looking out of his window. "Though that can't be it. It's too small."

But Erika was bringing the helicopter down on a bare patch of earth among wild grass and bushes. Ben and Zoe jumped down and gazed at their desolate surroundings. Erika appeared at their side. She pulled a remote control from her jacket and pressed a button. Sheets of old wood suddenly rose from the ground around the helicopter and made a shelter. A corrugated roof slid up from one of the walls and slammed down on top.

"Now no one will know there's a helicopter there," she explained. "It's important for Wild to stay absolutely secret. Follow me and mind where you step." She dodged round a pile of droppings. "There's 'fuel' everywhere."

She led the way through what looked like a chicken farm. There were tatty henhouses and chickens running about freely.

"It looks a mess," said Erika, "but that's all

part of Wild HQ's disguise. And I promise you the chickens are well looked after."

"Look at the chicks!" cooed Zoe, stopping to watch a mother hen stalk past, followed by her brood. "They're just like little balls of fluff!"

"Gooey overload." Ben pretended he was being sick.

Zoe stuck out her tongue at him, as Erika flung open the door of a rickety shed. There was an old-fashioned toilet inside. "In we go!" she said cheerfully. Ben and Zoe exchanged a look. They knew what each other was thinking. This was getting seriously weird.

It was a tight squeeze, especially after Erika had pulled the door shut and drawn the bolt across. She pulled the chain. Instead of the expected noise of water gurgling, there was a gentle hum. "Hold on to your bellies," she warned. "This is a turbo lift."

"Turbo's not the word!"
gasped Ben, as the lift
suddenly shot down and
finally came to rest deep
underground. "That was
better than any theme
park ride."

"Welcome to Wild,"
said Erika, as she stepped
out of the lift. "These
are our headquarters –
where we coordinate all
our plans."

The children followed
her into a long, brightly-
lit corridor. They passed
doors on both sides. Erika
waved a hand. "These are
bedrooms, bathrooms,
everything we need to live
on an island…"

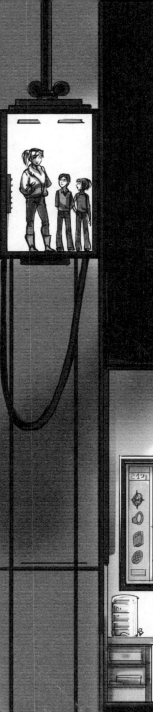

24

She stopped at a door at the far end marked Control Room and placed her fingertips on a pad.

"Print identification complete," came an electronic voice from the intercom above.

"This is like a spy film," Zoe whispered to Ben. "What are we letting ourselves in for?"

The door slid open. Erika ushered the children in and it closed silently behind them.

CHAPTER THREE

Ben and Zoe stared open-mouthed at the
huge, busy room in front of them. There
were people sitting at computers, who
looked up and smiled, then got back to
their work. The walls were covered with
giant plasma screens showing footage of
animals in the wild.

"They're all endangered," murmured Ben,
taking in the amazing sight of mountain
gorillas, pandas and hawksbill turtles in
their natural habitats. Zoe gasped and
pointed at one of the screens.

"That's the black-tailed ferret!" she exclaimed. "They're nearly extinct."

"You're right," came a deep voice. "Wild's working hard to stop that from happening."

Out from behind a workstation stepped a smiling Uncle Stephen. He was wearing old jeans and a dinner jacket with a bow tie. His spiky red hair looked as if it hadn't been brushed for days.

"Ben and Zoe!" He shook their hands vigorously. "You haven't changed much from the seven-year-old scamps I remember," he said. "There's always been a thirst for adventure in those bright blue eyes."

"It's great seeing you again," said Zoe, giving him a hug.

Uncle Stephen laughed and ruffled her hair. "What do you think of Wild headquarters?"

"They're awesome," said Ben, looking round the bustling room. "How deep underground are we?"

"A few hundred metres," Uncle Stephen replied. "It keeps us away from prying eyes. You'd be surprised how much space we have down here. Apart from this control room there are offices, living quarters, labs, a games room and even a swimming pool."

"I can't imagine you organizing all this!" Zoe grinned cheekily.

"You've got a point, Zoe," Uncle Stephen chuckled. "But thanks to Erika, Wild runs like clockwork. She's my second-in-command and keeps everything moving along smoothly. I just do a bit of tinkering here and there."

"I think you're being modest," said Erika. "After all, you are the driving force behind the entire operation and it's you who does all the planning of our missions."

"Well, I suppose there is that," admitted Uncle Stephen.

"And you invent all the gadgets and equipment Wild uses," Erika went on.

"All environmentally friendly, of course," put in Uncle Stephen.

"Like the chicken poo fuel," said Zoe. "What do you use the eggs for? Something really ingenious?"

"Breakfast." Their godfather grinned. "I like them boiled, with soldiers."

"There's one thing I don't understand," said Ben thoughtfully. "Why does Wild have to be secret? Couldn't you get more help if the organization was known?"

"We could," said Uncle Stephen. "But we'd get a lot more enemies, too. If nobody knows we exist we can operate in our own way."

"There are people out there who'd want to stop us helping endangered animals," explained Erika. "Poachers, collectors, those who have their own plans for the animals' habitats. So we must remain completely hidden from the world."

"As you can see, working for Wild can be dangerous at times," added Uncle Stephen, "but it's always very rewarding. Now are you ready to take on your first mission?"

"Mission?" Ben's eyes lit up. "Are we off somewhere else?"

"Of course," said Uncle Stephen. "Wild has a very important project and who better than my wonderful godchildren to undertake it!" He rubbed his hands eagerly. "One of Wild's planes will be ready first thing tomorrow. Erika will be your pilot again." He saw the stunned amazement on the children's faces. "You look like a couple of Kootenai sturgeon gawping at me like that." He chuckled.

Erika cleared her throat. "You haven't told them where they're going."

"Haven't I?" Uncle Stephen went over to a control panel and touched it. On the largest screen a world map appeared. He navigated it to the Indian Ocean and zoomed in on a long, thin island. "Sumatra," he said.

"Wicked!" exclaimed Zoe. "We've never been to that part of Asia."

"Your mission is to save a tiger," said Uncle Stephen. "We've named her Tora."

"Sumatran tigers are critically endangered," Ben piped up. "There's only a few hundred left living freely – mainly because of poaching. Body parts are used in traditional medicine and that's illegal."

"We know," hissed Zoe. "Stop showing off."

"Ben's right," said Uncle Stephen. He waved a hand towards a young man who was bent over a keyboard. "James over there is part of our team who intercept internet information about poaching."

James smiled and gave them a quick nod.

"He found out that poachers are active around Aman Tempat, a village in the south-west," Uncle Stephen continued. "Last month they killed a male tiger, probably Tora's mate. Now Tora is being targeted by a rich collector, a woman who'll pay these poachers handsomely for her capture – and for her two newborn cubs. But we've got a bit of time. According to the information we've gathered, they're waiting for the cubs to be old enough to come out of their den."

"When will that be?" asked Ben.

"Good question," said Uncle Stephen. "At a rough guess – with the information we've gathered about Tora – we think she had the cubs about six weeks ago…"

"Bet they're gorgeous!" Zoe sighed.

Her godfather nodded. "Indeedy, Zoe. Tiger cubs don't emerge from their den until they're two months old. And we don't want to interfere with this natural course of events if we can help it. Your mission is to monitor the den and alert us as soon as they do. Then we can rescue them before the poachers get hold of them."

"When the cubs are out, you'll make contact and we'll tell the nearby Kinaree Sanctuary," Erika added. "Anonymously, of course."

"And in the meantime, we'll try to find out more about this woman," said Uncle Stephen, looking stern for once. "She must be stopped."

"There's something I don't understand," said Ben. "Why are the poachers waiting for the cubs to come out of their den? Why don't they just get them now?"

"The poachers have a very special commission," said Dr Fisher solemnly. "The private collector wants the cubs to be a certain size. She's going to have Tora and her cubs killed – and stuffed."

"NOOO!" yelled Ben and Zoe.

"So you see how urgent this is. But keep well clear of those poachers. They're dangerous! Men like that will stop at nothing if they're paid well enough. Now, Erika, have I forgotten anything?"

"BUGs, Dr Fisher?"

The children exchanged puzzled looks.

"Of course!" said Uncle Stephen. "Silly me, you'll need your Brilliant Undercover Gizmos."

He flung open a drawer and began to hunt through it, pulling out pencil sharpeners, bits of old headphones and a half-eaten sandwich. "Got them!" he said, his face lighting up with excitement as he pulled out what looked like a couple of handheld game consoles. "My latest invention. Wonderful things. Solar rechargeable. Never let you down. They've got nearly everything you'll need in one

neat gadget – communicators, translator,
tracking devices. And they flick back to an
innocent game if anyone comes along." He
handed them to Ben and Zoe.

"Cool." Ben grinned, turning his BUG
over in his hand. It was made of hard shiny
black plastic with a small screen
and lots of buttons.

"We must also visit the storeroom," said Erika with a smile. "We have specially designed lightweight backpacks that we can fill with everything you need. Your gran said you're up to date with your travel jabs."

Ben nodded, but Zoe looked thoughtful.

"Let me get this right, Uncle Stephen," she said. "You want me and Ben to go to the other side of the world to save a tiger and her cubs from highly dangerous poachers."

"Got it in one!" declared their godfather. "You're perfect for the job. Who would suspect a couple of kids who appear to be on holiday? I knew you two were the ones I wanted because you're brave and clever and you know more about animals than anyone else I can think of. But most importantly I can trust you." Then he frowned and looked at them earnestly.

"Er … I suppose I should ask – will you do it?"

"YES!" shouted Ben and Zoe together.

CHAPTER FOUR

Zoe woke with a start. For a moment she couldn't think where she was. Then she remembered. Was it only two days ago they'd agreed to undertake the biggest adventure of their lives? And now here they were on the other side of the world – in a little wooden hut in the hot, steamy Sumatran rainforest. The excitement made her stomach flutter.

She flung her sheet off and swung her legs over the edge of the camp bed, tangling herself in the mosquito net that hung around it. At last she emerged, tousle-haired, and stared at the bed next to hers. Ben was fast asleep.

"Wake up!" she said, shaking him through his netting.

Ben muttered and turned over.

Zoe sighed. Ben always suffered worse jet lag than her whenever they travelled great distances. It had been dark when they'd arrived at the hut last night with Erika after a long plane ride and then a bumpy journey in a jeep. The hurricane lamp hadn't given off much light, but now bright sunshine was streaming in through the blinds. Zoe padded round the room, feeling the rough matting under her bare feet. The place was simple – a single room with a cupboard, a one-ring stove and a stone bowl in the corner.

Erika had left bottles of water and some fruit on a little table. She'd told them to tell anyone who asked that they'd come with their Aunt Erika, who liked to go off sightseeing on her own. Erika had certainly "gone off", but not sightseeing. By now she'd be in Jakarta, following a lead on the rich collector.

Zoe took a drink, pulled her crumpled clothes out of her backpack and got dressed. Grabbing a banana, she took her BUG outside. The hut was in a clearing a little way from the village of Aman Tempat. It was surrounded by lush green trees, and the air was full of birdsong and the scent of flowers. A blue winged butterfly landed on the log next to her. Zoe noted that the sun was directly overhead. It was midday. They must have slept for hours.

"What did Erika say about using the BUGs?" She scrolled down the menu. "Translator. How does that work?" There was a small button on the side. It was made

of a soft, squishy plastic and came away in
her hand. "Earpiece!" she exclaimed,
sticking it in her ear. It was so comfortable
she couldn't even feel it.

Inside the hut, Ben opened his eyes.
He could hear Zoe muttering outside.
"Communicator … satellite tracker…"

Good, he thought, scrambling out of bed.
Zoe's finding out about the BUGs. Ben loved
gadgets, but he was too impatient to learn
how to use them. Zoe was doing all
the investigating and that
suited him.

"Morning!" He
popped his head
round the
curtain.

"Afternoon, you mean!" Zoe grinned. "This BUG's fantastic. I'm trying to remember everything Erika told us about it. It's no use asking you – I could see you weren't listening to anything she said."

"I *was* listening," said Ben. "Well, a bit, anyway. I remember her saying we have to pretend to be on holiday, and the local people are used to tourists … and … and…"

"And that was it," said Zoe. "You were either fiddling with the TV on the plane or eating."

"One of those TV programmes told me a lot about Sumatra," Ben argued.

Zoe didn't have an answer for this so she stuck out her tongue at him. "Get dressed," she said. "We've got to go into the village and find out as much as we can about Tora. And we might get a mobile signal there. I can't get one here. We must be out of range.

But remember to be careful. No one must
know what our mission is."

"My mission is to buy food," insisted Ben.

"You would think of your stomach first!"
Zoe laughed.

Ben dressed quickly and they followed a
narrow path, soon emerging into a little
marketplace surrounded by houses. All the
houses had steeply curved roofs with carved
points at each end. Several of them had
shopfronts. The place was bustling.
Villagers called to them to come and see
what they were selling.

"Erika was right," Zoe whispered to Ben.
"They're used to tourists."

"They must be speaking Bahasa
Indonesia," Ben whispered back. "That's the
local language."

"No, it's English," said Zoe, with a smile.

"It's not!" snorted Ben. "I can't
understand a word."

"Perhaps you should wash your ears out!" said Zoe solemnly. "The lady at that stall with the bamboo baskets is saying she has rice, fish and fruit – best in the village. Why aren't you there buying some? You said you were hungry."

Ben just looked confused. Zoe burst out laughing. Making sure no one was watching, she grabbed his BUG and pulled off the earpiece that was hidden there. "Sorry, couldn't resist. You were right. The language *you're* hearing is Bahasa Indonesia. And this is a translator. I've got mine in already. It makes the voices a bit electronic, but I can understand everything they say. Stick it in your ear. Never know what we might find out. But remember, don't let on."

"Lead me to the food!" declared Ben, shoving in the earpiece. "What's that awesome smell? It's coming from that shop over there." He pointed to a large hut with wooden walls and a tin roof. The front was crammed with a hotchpotch of goods – tins and belts next to T-shirts and jars of coffee and sweets.

A man was crouched over a small stove at the front. He was frying something in a pan. Ben grabbed Zoe's arm and dragged her towards it.

The shopkeeper looked up. "Banana fritters," he said in English, giving Ben and Zoe a broad grin. "We call them *godok pisang.*"

"Don't need your clever translator here," Ben muttered in Zoe's ear. He pulled out the wallet of rupiah that Erika had given them. "Five please."

"Just one for me," added Zoe.

"You are Australian?" asked the stallholder, ladling the sizzling fritters into a small bamboo bowl. He spoke with a strong accent.

"No, we're from England," explained Zoe. "On holiday," she added quickly. "With our aunt."

The man nodded. "We have many visitors from Australia," he told them. "Not so many from England. I am pleased to meet you. My name is Catur."

"I'm Ben," said Ben with his mouth full.

"This is my sister Zoe, and this is a fantastic fritter!"

"It's nice here," Zoe told the shopkeeper. "We can't wait to explore."

"There are good bus rides," Catur told them. "My brother-in-law is the driver. You can go as far as Gonglung. It's a big town."

"And what about this jungle?" said Ben, pointing at the dense wall of trees around the village. "We want to see some wildlife."

"Too dangerous to go on your own," said Catur. "Tell your aunt to keep you away from there. There are fierce animals in the jungle, clouded leopards, many wild cats, even a tiger."

Zoe nudged Ben's ankle with her foot. "A tiger?" she gasped. "We'll definitely keep away!"

"Does it come near the village?" asked Ben.

"If it did you would not be in danger," said Catur. "We would set a trap."

Zoe started at this. "And kill it?" she blustered.

"No." Catur smiled. "It would be taken to the Kinaree Sanctuary. It is a good place for tourists to see. Your aunt could take you. It is only a day's drive from here. Now, is there anything else you need? I have necklaces, scarves, many nice things for you to take home."

Zoe shook her head. "We'll come back later. Thanks for the *godok pisang*."

As they carried on through the village, they saw a man sitting outside on a veranda, drinking from a bottle. He wore a battered baseball cap and ragged trousers. He watched them coldly, rocking his chair on its back legs.

"He looks scary," muttered Zoe.

At that moment, three other men came up the steps of the veranda. The ragged-looking man jumped up, glanced round suspiciously and opened his door to usher them inside. The men all removed their shoes. Zoe turned up her BUG and listened to the translated conversation.

"Got to keep it quiet, Wicaksono!" one of the newcomers was saying as he made for the door. "No one must find out – especially my wife. She'll be really angry if she finds out what we're doing, even though there's a lot of money in it."

"Money for *me*," laughed the ragged man. "I'm the one who's going to make a killing!"

The wooden door of the hut slammed behind them.

Zoe and Ben walked away to a safe distance. Zoe turned to her brother. "He talked about making a killing and getting lots of money for it. Do you think that Wicaksono man could be our poacher?"

"I reckon you could be right," said Ben. "And what is he most likely to be hunting?"

"Tora!" exclaimed Zoe, horrified.

CHAPTER FIVE

"So we've found our poacher," said Zoe, squatting under the shade of a palm tree in the marketplace. "I know Uncle Stephen said we had to stay away from poachers, but there's nothing to stop us just keeping an eye on Wicaksono's activities. We need to know what danger Tora's in, don't we?"

"Is there something on the BUG that tracks animals?" said Ben.

"Of course," said Zoe, with an air of mock patience. "If you'd been listening to Erika, you'd know we can dart Tora with a tiny microchip. She'll hardly feel it. She'll probably think it's an insect bite. But that doesn't help us now."

Ben grinned mischievously.

"Wait a minute," said Zoe. "What are you planning? I can always tell you've got some crazy idea when you get that gleam in your eye."

"We fire a tracking dart into Wicaksono," said Ben, smiling broadly. "Then we can follow him and find out what's going on!"

"Someone's coming out," hissed Zoe. She dragged Ben off between two of the houses.

They could just see the men talking on the veranda.

Ben got out his BUG and tapped in "tracking".

"I see you've got the hang of it at last!" whispered Zoe.

Ben didn't answer. A target ring was showing on the screen.

Holding it up, he focused on Wicaksono's bare arm. Click! Ben fired a dart. Immediately the man flinched and clutched his arm. Then he looked round angrily.

"Keep out of sight," muttered Ben. "If he sees us he might be suspicious!"

Wicaksono cursed and slapped his arm.

"He thinks it's a mosquito," said Zoe in relief.

The man waved his friends off and went back inside the house.

Ben checked the screen. A satellite map of Aman Tempat came up and a green light pulsed just where Wicaksono's house was.

"It'll flash to warn us if he leaves the village," he said.

"What are you doing?" came a translated voice in their earpieces. They looked up guiltily, then quickly pretended they had not understood. Zoe clicked the screen of her BUG to game mode.

It was the woman who had been calling from her stall. She stared at them and the BUG, puzzled. Then she grinned.

"You same as my young brother."

She chuckled. She spoke in halting English now. "Play on computer all the time. Where your parents? I have food to sell."

"We're with our aunt. She's away for the day," said Zoe. "But we'll buy some food."

The woman beckoned to them and they followed her to her stall.

"We're on holiday," Zoe told the woman, while Ben eagerly inspected the baskets of brightly-coloured fruits. She patted her chest. "I'm Zoe." Then she pointed at Ben. "This is Ben, my brother. We're twins."

"I'm Angkasa," said the woman. She pointed upwards. "It means the sky."

"We're desperate to explore," said Zoe. "But people say the jungle is not safe."

She was hoping the woman might know more about Tora than Catur seemed to.

Angkasa nodded. "Many stories about the jungle. There is creature called *orang pendek*." Angkasa took on a fearful look.

"People say he is small man – hairy and strong like five elephants. My father saw one but not me."

"Wicked," said Ben, forgetting about the food for a moment.

"My father saw it at Silent Water," Angkasa went on. "It is watering hole in the jungle." She shivered. "We not go there. Evil place."

"Do animals use it?" Zoe asked, glancing at Ben.

"Yes," said Angkasa. "But not people. Even poachers keep away, I think."

"Poachers!" exclaimed Zoe.

Angkasa nodded. "Not welcome in village. There was tiger eating our goats. We told Kinaree Sanctuary and got trap ready. We always do this. Sanctuary comes and takes tiger to safe place. But poachers got there first. Someone in village helped them."

"Someone in the village?" gasped Zoe, pretending to be shocked by the revelation.

Angkasa lowered her voice. "Bad man." Her eyes flickered down the row of houses. Zoe was sure that she was looking at Wicaksono's house. "He sells bones, skin, whiskers. Against the law."

She looked around suddenly as if she thought she might be overheard.

"I have work," she said hurriedly, finding bags for the food Ben had chosen.

Ben and Zoe paid and set off for their hut. They said nothing until they were well away from the village.

"We're as good as spies!" Ben laughed, punching Zoe's arm. "We've pinpointed the poacher, and we know where to start our search for Tora. Where she must go to drink and hunt – Silent Water."

"And we've done it all in one afternoon," said Zoe, rubbing her arm. "Uncle Stephen will be proud of us."

"Yes," said Ben, as he scrolled through the menu on his BUG and brought up a map of the area. "Silent Water's here," he murmured. "Looks like it's the only water around so it would be the place where all the animals drink. Tigers like to drink at night so that's when we'll go there."

"It's a good place to start," agreed Zoe, "but I don't like the sound of it. What did she call that strange hairy man?"

"*Orang pendek*." Ben grinned. "It's just a story. Like the Loch Ness monster, or Bigfoot. Anyway, I'll look after you."

"You?" scoffed Zoe. "You'd be as much use as a concrete trampoline."

"Then don't come running to me when the creature bites your legs off!" joked Ben. He ducked as Zoe swiped at him.

"Anyway, how's our poacher doing?" she asked.

"Still at home," said Ben, glancing at his BUG. "We haven't got to worry about him till the cubs come out."

"And we've got an advantage," said Zoe. "The poachers have no idea we're going to thwart their plans. Wild to the rescue!"

BUG SAT MAP

JUNGLE

COCHO
HI

BASE
CAMP

CATUR'S
SHOP

MARKET PLACE

WICAKSONO'S
HOUSE

AMAN TEMPAT

SILENT
WATER

JUNGLE

TRAIL

N

NOT TO SCALE

CHAPTER SIX

"What time is it?" asked Ben as they sat on the floor of their hut, eating fish and rice from a papaya skin.

"17.30," said Zoe. "It'll be dusk soon. And darkness comes very quickly this near the equator."

"Tiger-tracking time!" said Ben. "Tigers are mainly nocturnal and usually hunt at night."

"Thank you, Mr Walking Encyclopedia." Zoe laughed.

Ben threw his papaya skin into the bin

and pulled on his walking boots. "Let's go!"

"Hang on a minute!" said Zoe. "Don't forget your water bottle." She unzipped a small backpack from her big one and put water, fruit and the medical kit inside. Then she checked the route on the BUG's satellite map. "We'll need the night vision glasses Erika told us about. It'll get pitch black under the trees." She plunged her hand into one of the backpack pockets. "I think they're in here somewhere."

"Can't we put them on when we need them?" said Ben impatiently.

"Silly!" said Zoe, pulling out two pairs of small, lightweight goggles on a thin strap. "It'll be so dark we'll need night vision glasses to find the night vision glasses."

"These are state-of-the-art technology," exclaimed Ben. "Remember the huge ones Mum and Dad used when they were looking for that injured elephant in Botswana?"

"They made them look like aliens!" Zoe laughed.

Ben pulled his over his head. He opened the door to the hut and stared out into the gloom. "The world's gone green," he said. He twiddled a dial on the nosepiece. "Awesome. They've got telephoto lenses. I can zoom right in."

He stepped out of the hut and into the darkening jungle.

"This is going to be hard work," he said,

```
2.25
phts

bat: 6.5


autonomy
high
```

21 h 256B light 66.54

pushing aside branches to make a way
between the trees. As their footsteps
crunched on the mass of ferns and dead
leaves of the forest floor they heard the
warning cries of animals deep among
the trees.

"The BUGs have got scent dispersers,"
hissed Zoe, as she clambered over a fallen
tree trunk. "Activate them. That way we
won't smell like dinner to anything lurking
in here."

"Too right." Ben grinned. "You don't want to scare Tora away with your pong!"

"She'd already have seen your ugly mug and scarpered!" Zoe retaliated. "Now shush. We've got a job to do."

They moved on, keeping their footsteps as quiet as possible. After a while, Zoe stretched up and ran her hand over the bark of a tree.

"There's no time for nature studies!" Ben told her.

"But this is important," insisted Zoe. "Look."

Four deep vertical gashes ran down the trunk, showing the light wood beneath.

"Wow," gasped Ben. "Tiger score marks." He sniffed at them. "They look fresh. Did you know that's what tigers do to mark their territory and warn others off?"

"Of course." Zoe sighed. "And I know this as well – they've got to be Tora's. Erika said she's the only tiger in the area." She looked around. "Her footprints must be here somewhere."

"Pugs, you mean," said Ben smugly.

There was a sudden animal shriek from high in the trees. They froze. Zoe's BUG vibrated in her hand.

"Phew!" she whispered. "It's analyzed the sound. It was just a tarsier monkey."

They walked on, carefully watching every movement from the undergrowth, pausing when a spiny little creature scurried past. "Brush tailed porcupine," Zoe told Ben. "Wish we had time to study the wildlife."

They came to a sort of corridor through the trees, where large animals had broken away the vegetation to make a path. Ben bent to examine the ground.

"We're on her trail," he said in excitement. "I've found a faint pug mark. This must be the way she comes to drink."

Zoe joined him. There on the soft earth was a large indent and four smaller ones.

"I thought they'd be more like circles," said Zoe, puzzled.

"That's the males," said Ben. "Female tigers have uneven pads. It's got to be Tora's!"

Zoe checked her satellite map. "Looks like this path heads straight to Silent Water. Cool! We're taking the same track as her."

They followed the trail through the trees for almost an hour, heading deeper into the jungle. Zoe suddenly clutched Ben's arm.

"What is it?" hissed Ben.

"Dunno," said Zoe. "I've just got a sort of creepy feeling. Remember what Angkasa said about Silent Water. Supposing that orang thingy shows up."

Ben grasped her by the hand and pulled her along. "There won't be anything like that there," he said, sounding braver than he felt. "It's just a story."

A screech split the air and echoed eerily round. "It's a macaque," said Ben quickly, as he felt Zoe tense and pull back. "We've heard them before in Thailand, remember. Hey, I can see water through the trees. Better be quiet. She may already be there."

The trees gave way to a large clearing. In front of them was Silent Water, flat and smooth, glimmering in the moonlight. It was surrounded by tall, overhanging trees and a tangle of bushes. A fallen tree rested in the pool and large rocks were scattered about the bank. There was no sign of the tiger.

"How weird," muttered Zoe, glancing nervously round at the branches that arched like giant fingers over the water.

"It really *is* silent. There must be animals around here, but it's like everything's just … frozen."

Suddenly they could hear something moving through the trees on the other side of the waterhole. Zoe dragged Ben down behind a thick, ferny bush to the side of the trail. "What's that?" she whispered.

A solid black shape barged into the clearing, with a cracking of branches underfoot. The moonlight caught its leathery back.

"If that's an *orang pendek*, I'm a dung beetle," hissed Ben.

"It's a Sumatran rhino," gasped Zoe, her fear forgotten. "They're so rare. There's hardly any left in the wild. Look at his cute little face."

"They might look cute, but they can be dangerous," warned Ben. "If that charged at you it'd be like being hit by a car."

They watched as the heavy, slow-moving rhinoceros lowered its head to the water. Its long, hairy ears twitched as it drank.

"To think it's killed for its horns," Zoe whispered. "We must tell Uncle Stephen that there are some here."

Gradually Silent Water came alive. Deer, wild pigs and tapirs emerged with their families to drink and swim. Zoe checked the time. To their amazement, two hours had passed since they'd arrived at the waterhole.

"I'm getting numb feet," moaned Ben. "I've never stayed still for so long."

"Maybe Tora doesn't come here after all," said Zoe, stifling a yawn.

"Can't give up yet," said Ben. "Let's take turns to sleep. You first."

"I'll never nod off out here," protested Zoe, leaning against a tree trunk.

The next thing Zoe knew she was being
shaken awake.

"Don't say anything," whispered Ben.
"Something's happening."

All the animals were standing alert.
There was a faint rustling from the path.

Whoosh! In an instant the animals fled
as a sleek dark shape stepped out into the
clearing. It moved steadily along in the
dark, proud head held high and muscles
rippling. The silky fur, with its distinctive
narrow stripes, gleamed in the faint
moonlight.

"It's Tora," breathed Ben.

"She's beautiful." Zoe sighed.

Tora padded silently towards the water, the black tip of her long tail curling up behind her.

All of a sudden, she stopped and sniffed the air. With a low growl she came straight for their hiding place.

They heard a sound like water spraying and a pungent smell filled the air. Then they felt a trickle of warm, stinky urine squirting over them through the bush. Tora was leaving her scent!

At last she finished and moved off towards the water.

"Gross!" gasped Ben under his breath.

"At least we know the scent disperser works!" whispered Zoe, trying not to make a sound as she wiped herself down on a leaf. "She didn't know we were here."

"Wish it worked both ways," Ben whispered back. "That stinks!"

They peered through the leaves at Tora, who was now further along the bank. She plunged into the water and swam strongly, head held high. Then she got out, shook herself and began drinking deeply at the edge of the water.

"I expect she'll go hunting next," said Ben. "She'll have to take food back to the cubs. They'll be having a mixture of meat and mother's milk at six weeks."

"If we follow her, she should lead us to her den," agreed Zoe. "Then we'll know where to go to check on the cubs."

Ben picked up his BUG. "I'll dart her."

He targeted Tora and fired at her left haunch. Pfft! The tiger's skin rippled and she flicked her tail as if she was swatting a fly. Immediately, a satellite map of Silent Water showed on the screen and an orange light started flashing, showing the exact position of the tiger.

"What's that?" Zoe parted the leaves again. "There's something moving by Tora's legs." She put her goggles to zoom. "It's too blurry to make anything out." She adjusted her focus. Now she could see clearly.

Two little cubs were playing at the tiger's feet, padding each other and rolling together at the edge of the water. Ben gave a low whistle. "Uncle Stephen's got his dates wrong. It's Tora's cubs. They're older than we thought. They're out."

"Then they're in terrible danger," said Zoe. "And it's up to us to save them."

CHAPTER SEVEN

"Check where the poacher is," whispered Ben urgently. "If he's on to this we've got to stop him."

"He's not moved from the village," answered Zoe, checking the green light. Then she put her BUG into communication mode.

"We must tell Erika immediately," she murmured, as she pressed 2 – the hot key that would dial Erika direct. "No signal here!" She groaned in frustration. "I suppose there aren't many phone masts in the jungle."

"We can't get a signal from our hut and we don't want to risk being heard in the village with this news," said Ben, keeping his voice down. "We don't know who's in league with that poacher. We need to get higher."

"Well, I'm not climbing trees in the middle of the night!" declared Zoe.

"Don't worry," hissed Ben. "We'll just go to higher ground."

"OK," Zoe agreed. "But Tora will hear us if we leave now. We'll just have to wait till she goes."

"That's lucky for you," grinned Ben. "You can do some fluffy-wuffy little cub watching. I'm going to get some sleep."

Zoe eagerly trained her goggles on the cubs. "Oh but they're sooo sweet," she cooed softly. "Look at them suckling from their mum! Now one's biting the other one's ear. And listen to them mew, Ben.

I could just hug them."

Ben sighed and gave up trying to sleep. They watched Tora nudge her cubs towards the water. The cubs spluttered as they drank. Tora seemed to be keeping guard. She held her head high and gave off soft, deep growls.

"She's a good mum," said Zoe. "She'll guard those babies with her life."

"Freeze," warned Ben. "She's on the move."

Tora was padding silently towards the trail – and towards Ben and Zoe. They held their breath, hoping the scent dispersers were still working. Tora might be hungry. Zoe felt a mixture of thrill and terror as the beautiful tiger stalked along, her cubs padding at her heels. They looked as if they were trying to be as regal as their mother, but couldn't resist sniffing the ground or ambushing each other as they went. Zoe gave a regretful sigh as they disappeared.

"Let's go," said Ben, stretching his stiff legs. "No time to lose."

"First I'll find out exactly where the nearest high ground is," Zoe told him as she checked her screen. "We can't wait for ever for you to work it out … there it is. Cochoa Hill."

It was a long walk through the dark forest to Cochoa Hill. By the time they had begun to trek up the slope, the first glimmers of sun were beginning to filter through the trees.

"I hope we get a signal up there," panted Zoe, as she pushed through the huge flowers and ferny undergrowth of the steep slope. "The sooner Wild can contact the sanctuary the better." She stopped to check her BUG. "Nothing yet."

At last they reached the top of the hill. Ben wiped the sweat off his forehead and drained the last of his water.

"Got a signal!" yelled Zoe, sending a flock of bright yellow birds screeching into the air. "No, it's gone again – and we've run out of hill."

"Now it *is* time for tree climbing," said Ben grimly. He looped the strap of his BUG round his wrist and began to shin up the nearest tree, using the dangling creepers to pull on and ignoring the ants that were running over his arms. "I hope I don't have to go as far as the jungle canopy," he called down.

"Be careful," warned Zoe. "I don't want you falling on top of me."

As Ben climbed, the forest suddenly darkened and huge drops of water began to splatter down through the trees. Soon every other jungle sound was blotted out by the beat of the water on the canopy above.

Ben could feel the tree swaying under his weight as he gripped with one hand and fumbled for his BUG with the other.

Rainwater was streaming down the trunk, making it hard to hold on. *Hope this thing's waterproof*, he thought to himself as he struggled with the slippery buttons. At last he accessed the communicator, tapped in Erika's hot key and held the BUG to his ear. It rang and rang. He pressed 1 to get through to Wild headquarters instead. "Hello?" he shouted as he heard a faint voice. The signal seemed to be coming and going. "Uncle Stephen?"

No answer. Still holding the device to his ear, he tried to scramble higher, pushing on the spindly branches with his feet.

"Tora's cubs are out of the den," he shouted. "And the poachers are in the village – at least we think so. Can you contact the sanctuary for us?"

"Hello, Ben!" He could just hear his godfather's cheerful voice. "Bad signal. Say again?"

Ben heaved himself up as high
as he could. "Sanctuary needs to
come now!" he said. "The cubs
are—"

CRACK! The branch under
his foot snapped and he fell.

He grabbed wildly at the
trunk as he went. Wet twigs
slapped in his face and he felt
the skin being scraped from
his palms, but he couldn't
get a handhold.

Then, with a jerk, the
BUG strap around his wrist
caught on a branch and he
found himself swinging ten
metres above the ground.
His arm felt as if it was
going to be pulled out of
its socket. But at least
he'd stopped falling.

The BUG suddenly vibrated. "Ben?" It was Uncle Stephen's voice. He could hardly hear it over the thunderous sound of the rain. "Are you there? How's it going?"

Typical, thought Ben. *I'm hanging from a tree in a tropical rainstorm and now I get perfect reception!*

"Urgent message!" he shouted up to the BUG. "Tora's cubs are out of the den." He twisted about, legs flailing, desperately trying to find something to hold on to.

"Already!" he heard Uncle Stephen exclaim. "Tell me all about them. Have they got…?"

The BUG bleeped and went silent.

Ben managed to get hold of a creeper and hauled himself on to a branch. He unhooked the BUG and climbed down the tree as quickly as his bleeding hands would allow. Zoe had found a huge leaf to shelter under. Ben joined her, nursing his wounds.

"Are you OK?" she yelled over the sound of the pounding rain. "I heard some noises and I called up, but I don't think you heard me."

"I slipped a little." Ben grinned, showing her his palms.

"Nasty." She grimaced. "Did you speak to Uncle Stephen?"

"Briefly," Ben yelled back. "I just hope he got my message OK, and that the sanctuary will be on their way to get Tora before the poachers do."

Zoe swung her backpack off her shoulder and found the medical kit. She splashed water on his grazes and began to cover them with dressings.

"Better get back to the village," said Ben. "I think we should … *ouch!* … make sure that the poachers … *yow, Zoe, that stings* … aren't on Tora's trail yet."

It was late morning by the time Ben and Zoe reached the village. It had stopped raining and everywhere was steaming in the sun.

"At least the rain's washed the tiger wee off," said Zoe. "Now to work."

"Can't we get something to eat?" moaned Ben. "If anyone hears my stomach rumbling, they'll think the tiger's arrived in town."

"As soon as we've checked out the poachers," Zoe insisted. She took out her BUG and tapped some keys. A green light flashed. "That Wicaksono's still at home and we might be able to get close enough to hear something if we hang around."

They made for his house. There was no sign of anyone, but there was a row of men's shoes by the door. They could hear a voice coming from inside.

"Deal again. I'm feeling lucky. Get your money ready."

"Sounds like cards," said Zoe.

"Risky," said Ben. "The programme I saw said that gambling is forbidden in Sumatra."

A woman was walking briskly towards the house. Zoe and Ben quickly sat down and pretended to be playing games on their BUGs. They made sure their translators were on and their earpieces in. The woman didn't seem to see them. She marched straight up the steps.

"Sapto!" she called in an angry voice. "I know you're in there!" She thumped on the wooden door. "I'm staying here until you come out."

There was a shuffling from inside. The woman bashed on the door again. At last it opened. Wicaksono stood there.

"Ah... Hello, Ratu..." he said. "Your husband isn't here. I haven't seen him..."

"Out of my way!" Without another word, the woman pushed past and went inside the house. Ben and Zoe could hear yelling and the sound of things being knocked over. Then the woman reappeared, dragging a man along by his ear!

"Some husband you are!" she yelled, as she pulled him down the steps, sweeping up his shoes as she went. "You promise to stop gambling and what do I find…"

"I'm sorry, Ratu my love," the man was whimpering, as they went out of sight. "I was just about to win – I had the best cards ever. You could have had everything you wanted … *ow!*"

Two other men came to the door of the hut. They pulled on their shoes and scurried off sheepishly.

Ben looked at Zoe. "If they're dangerous poachers, I'm an aardvark!" he said. "It was just a secret gambling game. 'Making a killing' was a phrase, not what they were setting out to do. We're back to square one."

CHAPTER EIGHT

"What do we do now?" said Zoe.

"Angkasa knew about the poachers," answered Ben. "Maybe we can ask her a few more questions without frightening her off."

They set off through the village, but there was no sign of the fruit stall today.

"What have you done to yourself?" said a voice. It was Catur. He came out of his shop and took Ben's hands. He looked concerned.

"I … slipped over," said Ben.

"I can sell you something to make it

heal." Catur gestured towards his shop.
"Come inside."

Ben and Zoe followed him in. Beads and
brooches and carved wooden animals were
displayed on a long table, next to a row of
bottles containing richly-coloured powders
and pills. There were some pretty rings
displayed on the back wall, beside a
curtained opening. Zoe went over to have
a look. She knew Gran would like them.

Catur picked up a small pot of bright red
ointment. "This is a salve made from the
lipstick tree. It helps to keep wounds
clean." He opened the lid and let Ben sniff
at it.

As Zoe examined the rings she had a
sudden thought. Catur might know
something about the man that Angkasa
had mentioned. But how could she bring
up the subject of poaching without
explaining why they wanted to know?

"This ointment is very good," Catur was saying. "But if you are willing to pay a bit more I have something ... special ... in my storeroom." He gestured towards the curtain. "Guaranteed to heal those wounds quickly. I don't tell everyone about it, but I like you two."

Suddenly alarm bells started ringing in Zoe's head. There was a sly sound to Catur's voice. And what did he mean by "special"? She exchanged a quick glance with Ben. She could see he had the same suspicion as her. Was Catur the "bad man" Angkasa had told them about? Was he dealing in animal parts and making ointments out of tiger bones?

"We haven't got much money on us at the moment," she said. "So we'll stick with the salve."

"Of course," said Catur smoothly. "But do come back if you need anything ... else."

As soon as they'd left the shop, Ben pulled
Zoe into the gap between two of the
wooden houses.

"We'll certainly be back," he muttered.
"And sooner than he thinks."

"You've got that look again," said Zoe.
"What are you planning?"

"It sounds as if Catur could be linked to
the poachers," Ben told her. "But we must
make sure we've got the right man this
time."

"And how do you plan to do that?"
demanded Zoe. "We can't ask him."

"I'm going to get a look inside that
storeroom," said Ben. "Let's see if there's
another way in."

They crept along past compost heaps and
chicken runs until they came to the back of
Catur's shop.

"There's a door," said Ben. "Now here's your part in the plan. Keep him busy while I search."

"OK," said Zoe. "But be careful. Remember what Uncle Stephen said. The poachers are dangerous." She grinned. "I forgot to get a ring for Gran!" she said brightly. "See you in a minute." She darted off.

Ben waited until he heard Zoe's voice ringing out. "I can't decide," she was saying loudly. "Could you take them out the front so I can get a better look in the light?"

Ben gingerly opened the back door of the shop and crept in. The storeroom was hot and gloomy, lit only by a small, dirty window. There were shelves piled high with tins and packets. Ben inspected them. This was the ordinary stock for the shop. He pulled out some cans of baked beans to see if there was anything hidden behind, but he found only a few dead flies.

"The green one is nice…" He could hear Zoe chattering on.

He noticed a shabby chest of drawers in the corner. He pulled open the top drawer, wincing as it squeaked. It was full of jars and boxes. Ben picked up a small glass bottle, containing what looked like strands of wire. Then he opened a box and nearly dropped it in shock. It was full of dried eyeballs!

Gross! he thought. *And that wasn't wire. It was whiskers.*

He opened the second drawer. There was something rolled up in brown paper, like a small rug. He uncurled an edge and found himself staring at a beautiful orange and black striped pelt.

Then he heard a muttered voice from the shop.

"I want to talk to you, Catur! Come with me."

The translated words rang in his ear. That wasn't Zoe. It was a man and footsteps were approaching! They were heading across the wooden floor of the shop – straight towards the storeroom. There was no time to get out. Ben squeezed into the tiny gap between the chest of drawers and the wall as the curtain was flung aside. Too late he realized he'd left the drawer open.

"You shouldn't be seen here," he heard Catur snap.

"I wouldn't be here if you'd told me

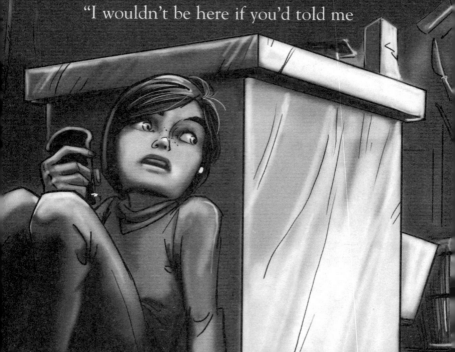

what's happening." It was the other man again. "When we didn't hear from you we started to think you were planning to do the job yourself and take all the money." He gave a cold laugh. "Then we'd have had to … see to you as well as the tiger."

Ben listened intently.

"You're crazy." Catur laughed coldly. "How could I cheat you, my friend? We're all in this together … we're like brothers. Meet me at the usual place at nightfall and I'll tell you the plan. Now go."

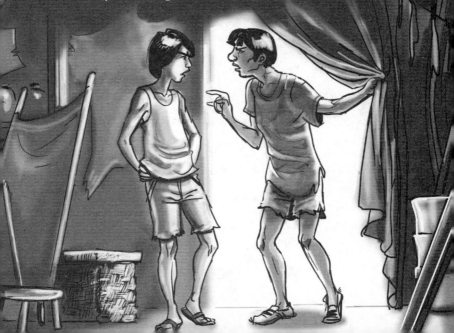

And we're going to be there to hear it, too, thought Ben.

He heard the stranger barge his way out of the back door. Then with horror he realized that Catur was coming over to where he was hiding. He tried to edge further back, but there was nowhere to go. He was going to be caught. Thump! Catur slammed the drawer shut then stomped back into his shop. Ben sagged with relief. He eased himself out of his hiding place, peered round the door to make sure the coast was clear, and slipped outside.

He sauntered round to the front of the shop. "Hurry up, Zoe," he called, pretending to be annoyed.

Zoe bounded out to join him. "Is he a poacher?" she whispered.

Ben nodded. "And we're going to follow him tonight and find out his plans."

"Stake-out time." Zoe grinned. "That

mango tree looks shady. We could spend the afternoon there."

"Mango," said Ben. "Delicious. Lead me to it!"

The sun was low over the trees when Catur locked up his shop. He hurried along a path towards the forest. Zoe quickly aimed the tracker, but Ben put his hand on her arm. "Too risky," he said. "We can't do anything that might alert him. He's sharp, this one."

Keeping to the shadows, they set off in pursuit, following the poacher's bobbing flashlight. It was dark by the time he came to a rough hut, half covered in vines. Ben and Zoe crouched down behind a pitcher plant, its large, cup-like leaves heavy with water. They slipped on their night goggles and put in their earphones so that they could hear the conversation translated. Two men were waiting for Catur on the veranda.

"That tall one with the big nose was the man in the shop," whispered Zoe. "He looks mean."

"And the short one's not much better," Ben replied. "We've got to be ultra careful."

As soon as the men had gone inside the hut, Ben and Zoe crept up and hid under a window.

"I've been to the den," came Catur's voice. "It was empty. So the cubs are out. This is the moment we've been waiting for. We must act quickly before any goody-goody sanctuary gets wind of it."

"Then we'll do it tonight." This was Big Nose. "Our client doesn't want to be disappointed."

"She won't be." Catur sounded sure of himself. "We'll place the trap at Silent Water – the tiger always drinks there. I've dug a hole ready to put it in. Then we'll come back here and wait in comfort. The trap has an electronic lock. The moment it's sprung, an alarm goes off on my remote. And there's no danger that any other creature will be tempted by the goat we'll use as bait – I got some of the tiger's dung from the empty den and smeared it on the skin of the male we killed last month. We'll hang it right by the trap. That should put off any other animals. They'll not risk running into a tiger."

"Why don't we lie in wait for her?" This was Shorty speaking. "We don't want to miss her."

"Don't be stupid," scoffed Catur. "She'd smell us before we even knew she was there. No, my friends, this is the way. We trap them then shoot them. A tiger in a cage is an easy target. But be careful where you aim. We don't want to damage the skins!"

Ben and Zoe gazed at each other in horror.

CHAPTER NINE

"They're killing the tigers tonight," whispered Zoe. "The sanctuary won't get here in time."

"That was a clever idea of yours, Catur, putting out scary stories about Silent Water," Big Nose was saying. "How did you dream that up?"

"I didn't have to," Catur replied. "There have always been legends about Silent Water." He gave a chuckle. "I just stirred things a bit. Believe me, the villagers would rather eat their own feet than go there after dark."

"You've never seen anything there, have you?" Shorty's voice sounded a bit shaky.

"Never!" scoffed Catur. "Are you bottling out?"

"Course not."

Ben's stomach gurgled loudly.

"Be quiet!" warned Zoe.

"I can't help it," insisted Ben in a low voice. "I'm hungry. We've missed a few meals today."

He began to fidget.

"What are you doing now?" muttered Zoe.

"I've got an apple in here." Ben plunged his hand in his pocket. "That'll keep… Oops."

The apple tumbled out and bounced loudly on the wooden veranda and into the long grass.

Ben and Zoe froze.

"What was that?" came a gruff voice from inside the hut.

"Is there someone outside?"

"If there is they'll be sorry!"

Chairs were scraped back and heavy footsteps made for the door.

"Run!" hissed Zoe.

They jumped off the veranda and into the bushes. The three men were out of the hut now, flashing torches around, guns in hand. Ben and Zoe tried to go deeper among the ferns, but it was impossible to move without making a noise.

"There. Can you hear it?" It was Catur. He moved his light over the leaves. The beam swept just above their heads. Ben felt something on his boot. He looked down and stifled a gasp – a coral snake was slithering silently over the laces. He closed his eyes and held his breath. *Think of something else*, he thought, sweating. *You must stay still*. But all he could think about was that the venom of the coral snake was deadly. He had to look.

Its tail was disappearing into the undergrowth. Ben let out a ragged breath.

"Over there!" shouted Catur. "I heard something."

Catur fixed his flashlight firmly on the bushes in front of them.

"Got an idea," hissed Zoe urgently, tapping some keys on her BUG. "Bring up the call and holo-image of the tarsier monkey." A shrill cry filled the air.

Ben looked up to see a holographic image of a tarsier projected high into the trees. He fumbled with his BUG. "Can't find it!"

Zoe snatched his BUG. Her fingers flew over the keypad. Then she thrust it back in his hands. Another piercing cry rose up and a second "monkey" appeared.

"What is that?" Big Nose was looking all about him.

"Tarsiers," said Catur, swinging his flashlight up into the trees. "They're all around here. Look."

Big Nose swung round with his gun and took a shot at the "monkey" in the tree.

"Don't waste your ammo," said Catur. "Save it for the tigers."

Zoe bit down a gasp. These men were despicable.

"Come on." Catur had his back to them now. "Let's get the trap in place."

The poachers trudged away to their shack. They reappeared carrying a large metal cage between them and set off. Soon the forest went back to its usual drone of insects and distant animal cries.

"That was a brilliant decoy, Zoe," said Ben. "Let's get after them. We've got to spring the trap before Tora gets there with her cubs."

"That won't work," said Zoe. "It'll set off the poachers' alarm and bring them running. They'll just come and reset it." She checked the tiger's whereabouts on her BUG. "She's a long way off at the moment and not moving. She's due south of Silent Water and we're here, look, to the west."

Ben nodded. "Then we get into her path

and scare her off before she gets anywhere
near the trap."

They hadn't gone far when Zoe suddenly
stared in horror at her BUG screen.

"Tora's on the move. She's going to get to
the trap before we can head her off."

"Then we've got no choice," said Ben.
"We have to get to the trap no matter what
the poachers do." He stopped in his tracks.
"But we won't spring it – we'll block it!
We should be able to get there before her.
We're nearer than she is."

"Brilliant!" said Zoe.

"That's me." Ben grinned.

They plunged through
the forest towards the
watering hole, twigs
cracking loudly
underfoot.

"Hope the poachers can't hear us," panted Zoe as they ran.

"We'll just have to take that chance," said Ben. "Look – we're here now. And I think the men have gone."

They made their way into the clearing. There was a sudden, sharp cry from across the pool. The children stepped quickly back into the undergrowth and Ben set his glasses to zoom.

"It's OK," he breathed. "It's only a family of dholes." He could clearly see the thin, fox-like dogs lapping at the water's edge. "Where's the trap?" he muttered. He ran along the bank, scattering the dholes. He came to a criss-cross pattern of large and small pugs in the soft earth. "It must be near here. They'll have put it near the tigers' tracks."

They pushed aside bushes and ferns, desperately searching for the trap.

Ben came to a mass of creepers. As he pulled at them his foot clanged against something hard and metallic.

"Found it," he called.

He knelt down and carefully removed some of the leaves. Underneath was a cage made of shiny sheet metal, set in the ground. The barred door was raised, ready to drop. He could hear the plaintive bleat of the goat inside.

Zoe joined him. Then something caught her eye. "Look, Ben!" she said. She pointed towards a huge tiger skin that had been draped over a nearby branch. "That's what Catur meant about putting other animals off. They'll all steer clear of that – especially if it's got Tora's scent all over it. That man is evil."

She checked the orange light on her BUG. "Oh no," she said urgently. "She's almost here. We've got to block the trap now."

They looked about.

"There must be some fallen branches we can lay across the opening," said Zoe, scanning the ground in panic.

"No time."

"Then we have to spring the trap after all and chase Tora away," cried Zoe.

But then, out of the corner of her eye, she caught a slight movement. She spun round. Tora was standing on the opposite bank, her cubs at her feet.

CHAPTER TEN

"Tora's here!" hissed Zoe, pushing Ben down into the undergrowth beside the cage. "I don't think she's seen us."

The tiger raised her head and sniffed the air, tail swishing.

"She can smell the goat," whispered Ben.

"And us, if we're unlucky!" Zoe pulled out her BUG. "Turn on your scent disperser."

The cubs suddenly bounded around the bank. With a low growl, Tora splashed through the water and overtook them. The tigers were making for the trap.

"We've got to do something." Zoe was almost in tears.

"There's only one thing for it!" cried Ben. Zoe could see he had that gleam in his eye which meant he was going to do something crazy. Before she could stop him, he had jumped into the metal cage.

CLANG! The trap slammed shut over his head.

At the harsh metallic sound, Tora reared up with a frightened snarl and the cubs leaped in terror. In an instant they'd disappeared into the shadows.

"It worked!" cried Zoe in relief. "Well done, Ben."

"Now get me out," called Ben as the goat nuzzled his ear. "The poachers will be here any minute."

Zoe pulled at the trapdoor. "I can't open it!" she said in alarm. "Try from the inside."

Ben pushed upwards. Nothing happened.

Zoe picked up a fallen branch and tried to lever the door open, but the branch snapped. She ran round the edge of the waterhole and found a sharp rock.

"Cover your face," she cried. "I'm going to smash the mechanism on top here."

She brought the rock down with all her strength. It shattered into fragments, leaving the locking mechanism barely scratched.

"I can't shift it," said Zoe in despair. "There must be something else I can do."

But it was too late. From the trees came the sound of raised voices. The poachers were on their way.

"Run, Zoe!" yelled Ben.

"I'm not leaving you!" declared his sister in horror.

"But you'll be caught too!"

"Shut up a minute," Zoe hissed. "I'm thinking what to do."

"No time!" Ben sounded frantic.

"Got it!" muttered Zoe. "This had better work."

She could see the torchlight flashing round the trees. Just as the poachers reached the clearing she slipped out of sight.

"Check the area," ordered Catur. "They might not all be in the trap."

"It's clear," came another voice. It was

Big Nose. "We've got the little beauties."
There was the click of a gun being cocked.
"Time to get rid of them."

"Good job they're quiet," commented
Shorty nastily. "Easier to kill."

Zoe pressed a button on her BUG. An
unearthly wailing sounded round the
clearing. Through a tiny gap in the creepers
she could see the men stop at the sound.
The barrel of a rifle was aimed straight at
her hiding place.

"What's that?" quavered Big Nose. He
looked frightened.

Beside him Shorty's gun was shaking as
he tried to keep it steady.

"Get on with it," snapped Catur. "That's
just some harmless animal. Don't waste time."

The men approached the trap with
nervous steps. Desperate now, Zoe set the
BUG wailing even louder. But it was no
use. Big Nose was crouching down, his gun

at his shoulder. Zoe knew that any minute he would see Ben.

Suddenly a deep rhythmic knocking sound came from the trap. Big Nose stumbled back, dropping his gun. "That's no tiger!" he gasped. "The locals were right. This place is evil."

"Don't be stupid," said Catur. "You're just getting spooked."

A dreadful groaning sound echoed inside the metal trap. Big Nose shone his torch down into it with a quivering hand. "Look at those huge shining eyes!" he gibbered. Then the words *orang pendek, orang pendek* rose in a ghostly howl.

"I can't stay here," yelled Shorty. "I'm off."

"Me too," wailed Big Nose.

Soon Catur was alone.

"Is this some kind of trick?" he muttered through gritted teeth, stalking towards the cage. "There's no such thing as an *orang pendek*." Zoe held her breath as he shone his torch through the grille. "What the—?" Catur sprang back in surprise. Then he laughed grimly. "Huge shining eyes?" he scoffed. "It's just a kid in goggles! Wait a minute. I know you!" He spoke in English now, and his voice had a murderous edge.

"You're in big trouble, boy." He released the trap mechanism and the door sprang open.

Zoe felt around until her hands closed on a heavy stick. Catur was not going to harm her brother – not if she could help it.

But a loud roar froze her to the spot. She saw Catur swing round to confront –Tora! The tiger was back. She stood on the bank, her hackles raised and her teeth bared. Catur gave a whimper. Tora crouched ready to spring as he aimed his gun.

"NO!" shrieked Zoe.

The sound of a bullet ripped through the air. Tora slumped to the ground, tried to raise herself up and fell heavily on to her side. Her tail swished weakly, her head sank slowly on to the muddy ground and she was still.

CHAPTER ELEVEN

The clearing was suddenly full of shouts and circling lights. The next moment Catur had vanished into the forest.

Zoe reached a hand out to Ben, tears streaming down her face.

"What's going on?" he gasped, as he clambered out of the trap, blinded by the strong flashlights. He tore off his goggles.

Zoe flung her arms round him. "I'm so glad you're OK!" she sobbed. Then she dropped to her knees and stroked Tora's lifeless body. "But we couldn't save this beautiful creature."

A woman ran up to them. She had an
Australian accent and wore a green uniform
with an elephant logo. "Whatever are you
kids doing here?"

Zoe looked at the woman, speechless. Ben
squeezed his sister's hand.

"We met a shopkeeper in Aman Tempat
who had some illegally poached stuff," he
explained. "He said his name was Catur.
We overheard him talking about killing a
tiger, so we followed him. We would've told

our aunt who's staying with us, but there was no time and we didn't know who else to trust. We managed to keep the tiger away from his trap…"

"…but we were too late to save her," Zoe sniffed.

"Too late?" said the woman. "What are you talking about? You can give yourselves a pat on the back. It wasn't too smart putting yourselves in danger, but it looks like you've saved this tiger's life."

Zoe gawped at her. "But the man shot her. She's dead."

"She's not dead!" The woman smiled. "That fool of a poacher never even fired his gun. Feel her chest. She's breathing."

"How come?" Ben was stupefied. "We heard a gun and she fell to the ground."

"That was me," said the woman. "I fired a tranquillizing dart at her." She held out a hand. "My name's Barbara. I'm with the

Kinaree Sanctuary. We got an anonymous message saying there was a mother tiger and cubs in danger. And they weren't the only ones. I didn't expect to find a couple of kids under fire as well!"

Zoe and Ben stroked Tora's magnificent fur. Now they were calmer they could feel her shallow breathing.

"Look at her noble face," said Zoe. "Her markings are so beautiful, the white around her muzzle and over her eyes."

"I don't get it," said Barbara, shaking her head. "We had no idea about this tiger and her cubs until we got the phone call. She must have kept herself well hidden."

"Where are the cubs?" said Ben suddenly.

"Barbara!" Someone called to the Australian. Ben and Zoe were astonished to see Wicaksono, the gambler from the village, carrying one of the cubs. Another man came behind with the second and a

third led the goat along on a length
of rope.

"We're lucky to have Wicaksono
here," Barbara said. "He's the
best animal trapper I know."

Ben and Zoe looked at each
other guiltily.

"You come see," Wicaksono
said in broken English, beckoning
to them.

Zoe and Ben didn't need to be told
twice. The cubs mewed and licked their
hands as they stroked their beautiful white
bellies. Wicaksono handed one of them
to Zoe.

"You hold," he said.

Zoe wiped her eyes on her sleeves and
took the tiger cub like a baby in her arms.
It was surprisingly heavy. "You're going to
be all right," she whispered as its big round
eyes gazed solemnly at her.

Four men came forward with a wooden cage pulled on a cart. The sleeping Tora was lifted very carefully and placed inside.

"Back to the village," said Barbara. "We'll come back for that horrible metal contraption later."

"What about this?" called a man, holding up the tiger skin in disgust.

"Bring that. We'll need it for evidence."

They all followed the cart. Wicaksono walked with Barbara, and they heard him asking questions about Tora's health. The first morning light was beginning to trickle through the trees.

"How could we have thought he was a poacher?" Zoe whispered to Ben as the little cub nuzzled her chin. "He loves animals."

"We shouldn't have jumped to conclusions so quickly," Ben agreed. "People aren't always how they seem. Catur seemed so nice when we first met him."

"Should we let Wicaksono know that we tagged him?" said Zoe.

"We can't," said Ben. "Then we'd have to tell him all about Wild. They seem to believe we're just tourists who stumbled across this horrible plot. It shouldn't do him any harm."

Back at the village, the wooden cage was winched on to the back of the sanctuary's truck. The cubs were put into a smaller box. Zoe and Ben stroked Tora's magnificent fur through the bars as she slept.

"Goodbye," said Zoe. "You're going to a lovely new home where you and your children can be safe."

Barbara came over to join them. "She'll need a name. Any ideas?"

They pretended to think. "How about Tora?" suggested Ben.

"Tora it is. And the cubs? They're a boy and girl."

Zoe opened her mouth.

"Don't you dare suggest Fluffy and Wuffy!" warned Ben with a grin.

"What are your names?" asked Barbara. "We'll name them after you."

"Ben and Zoe," they chorused.

"Perfect!" said Barbara.

"What happens next?" asked Ben.

"Our vet will do an examination and tag them, like you do dogs and cats," said Barbara. "Then they'll be set free in the reserve. Hopefully the mother will establish her territory and live a long and happy life. There's a male there already so she may have more cubs in time. Which is what we need if we're going to save the Sumatran tigers."

She turned, paid the villagers and got into the cab of the truck. Then she leaned out of the window, waving a notepad at Ben and Zoe.

"Stick your email address on here," she called. "I'll send you an update."

"And what about the poachers?" asked Zoe as she wrote. "There was Catur and two others, and they're still free."

"That shop over there is where Catur's selling animal parts," added Ben.

Barbara smiled. "I'll tell the police. Those villains will soon know what it's like to be hunted!"

With a throaty roar, the truck set off. Ben and Zoe watched until it had bumped out of sight in the early morning sunshine. Tora and her cubs were on their way to a safe new home.

"I hope they don't find our little tracking device when they examine Tora," said Ben, as they walked slowly through the market place.

"They'll never be able to work out where it came from." Zoe grinned. "You know what's really good?"

"Fish and chips," said Ben.

"No," said Zoe, giving him a friendly shove. "That collector will have to do without her family of stuffed tigers. I wonder if Erika's got any info on her."

"Hope she's been caught," said Ben through gritted teeth.

Zoe nodded. "That would be perfect. Course, we won't be able to put any of this on our website."

"It would make a great blog," agreed Ben. "It is a pity we've got to keep it all secret."

Zoe gave a huge yawn. "I need some sleep."

"And I need food!" added Ben. "I wasn't joking about the fish and chips." He pulled out his BUG. "I've got the hang of this now. We must let Uncle Stephen know about Tora." He pressed the hot key for Wild HQ.

"Hello, Ben." Uncle Stephen's voice came through loud and clear. "Is everything all right?" he asked. "Has our friend gone to her new home?"

"Yes," answered Ben simply. He was dying to tell his godfather every detail of the adventure but knew he couldn't risk being overheard. "Can't talk now."

"I understand." They could hear the happiness in Uncle Stephen's voice. "That's brilliant! I knew I could count on you. And Erika's had a successful mission, too. I'm sure she'll tell you all about it when she picks you up tomorrow. I'll see you back at HQ for a debrief." The connection was cut.

"Hope Uncle Stephen will give us a new mission when we see him," said Ben as they took the path to their hut. "Wonder what it'll be."

"I know one thing," said Zoe. "It'll be wild!"

TIGER SURVIVAL

95% of the worldwide tiger population has been lost in the last 100 years!

No. of tigers living in the wild today ——————→ about **4,000**
No. of tigers living in the wild 100 years ago ——————→ about **80,000**
No. of subspecies of tiger 100 years ago ——————→ **9**
No. of subspecies of tiger in the world today ——————→ **6**

Sumatran, Amur, Bengal, Indochinese, Malayan,
South China (there are possibly none of this subspecies left in the wild)

The
Sumatran tiger
is the smallest
subspecies of tiger.

Length
(from head to tail):
Male – 2.4 m
Female – 2.2m

Weight:
Male – 120kg
Female – 90kg

STATUS: CRITICALLY ENDANGERED

About **350** Sumatran tigers are thought to remain in the wild. They mostly live in the country's five national parks.

RESCUE

SUMATRAN TIGER FACTS

THREATS

POACHING

Killing tigers – and selling their body parts – is banned worldwide. However, this doesn't seem to be enough to stop tiger poaching, even though poachers know that if they're caught they face up to five years in prison and a very heavy fine.

Some tiger parts are said to have magical properties. The right front paw bone is thought to be the strongest. It is put into a glass of warm water. After a short while the water is drunk to treat headaches.

DEFORESTATION

Some areas of rainforest are logged illegally in order to sell the wood and land is often cleared for oil palm plantations. As its habitat disappears tigers cannot find enough prey and may stray into areas close to villages, where they risk being shot.

HUNTING

There are still people who hunt tigers for the pleasure of the kill.

It's not all bad news!

The **Sumatran Tiger Trust** is fighting for the future of the Sumatran tiger. It is funded by the South Lakes Wild Animal Park in Cumbria. Their tiger preservation team captures and re-releases tigers into safer areas. They send information on the location of Sumatran tigers to the Indonesian government, so it can forbid logging in areas where tigers have been found. The trust also tries to persuade loggers to leave 'corridors' of trees so that the tigers can move about from one forested area to another.

J. BURCHETT & S. VOGLER

WILD RESCUE

EARTHQUAKE ESCAPE

Following a massive earthquake, an orphaned giant panda has escaped from a sanctuary in China's Sichuan Province. Not only is he at risk of attack from leopards, but it seems he may have strayed into an area where all the bamboo has died. With the panda cub now in danger of starvation, it's up to Ben and Zoe to rescue him.

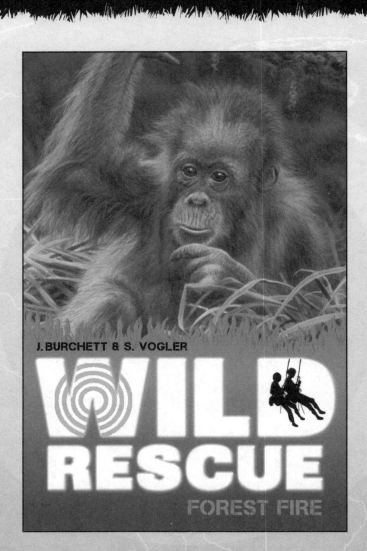

J. BURCHETT & S. VOGLER

WILD RESCUE

FOREST FIRE

Ben and Zoe's latest mission takes them to South Borneo. An orang-utan has set up home on a palm oil plantation and is resisting all attempts to bring him to the safety of the nearby reservation. But when they discover that illegal logging has been taking place, it becomes clear that the orang-utan isn't the only one in grave danger.

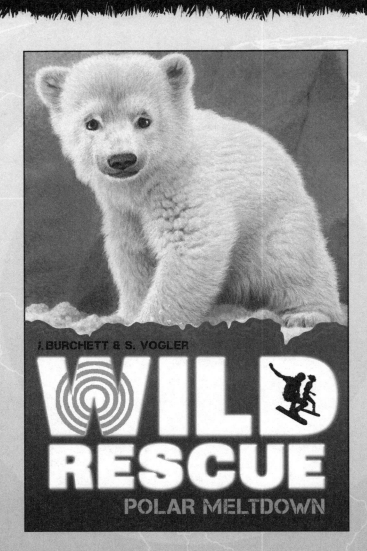

J. BURCHETT & S. VOGLER

WILD RESCUE

POLAR MELTDOWN

Following reports of a polar bear found dead near an Alaskan village, Uncle Stephen is sending Ben and Zoe to investigate. It is highly unusual for the animals to be found so close to human habitation. But the mission takes another turn when Ben and Zoe learn that the dead bear had recently given birth. This means there is an orphaned cub out there. Will they find it in time?

If you want to find out
more about tigers visit:

www.wildanimalpark.co.uk
www.tigertrust.info
www.wwf.org.uk